cocomelon™

PASTA PARTY!

Y0-BBW-411

Adapted by Patty Michaels

SIMON SPOTLIGHT
An imprint of Simon & Schuster Children's Publishing Division
New York   London   Toronto   Sydney   New Delhi
1230 Avenue of the Americas, New York, New York 10020
This Simon Spotlight edition December 2023
CoComelon™ & © 2023 Moonbug Entertainment. All Rights Reserved.

For information about special discounts for bulk purchases, please contact Simon & Schuster Special Sales at 1-866-506-1949 or business@simonandschuster.com.
Manufactured in the United States of America 1023 LAK
10 9 8 7 6 5 4 3 2 1
ISBN 978-1-6659-4761-9
ISBN 978-1-6659-4762-6 (ebook)

JJ is so excited! Today his grandma is cooking for him and his friends. They are having a pasta party!

Cece, JJ, and Cody can't wait to choose what pasta shapes, sauces, and toppings they would like to try.

♪ Pasta, pasta, pasta everywhere!
Pasta, pasta, pasta you can share. ♪

There are so many tasty choices!
Which ones will they pick?

🎵

Pasta, pasta, pasta everywhere!
Pasta, pasta, pasta you can share.
There's spaghetti, ravioli, fettuccine, or bow ties!
Pasta everywhere!
It's up to you—which do you like?

🎵

JJ and his friends look closely at the different pasta shapes. Everyone wonders what shape they should choose. There are so many choices!

Just then, JJ's grandma has an idea.
What if JJ chooses between just two shapes of pasta?

JJ thinks carefully. "I choose bow ties!" he cheers. Then JJ pretends to try on the piece of pasta like a real tie!

There's olive oil, marinara,
pesto, or alfredo white.
Pasta everywhere!
It's up to you—which do you like?

Now it's Cody's turn to
choose a pasta sauce.

Cody looks at the sauces curiously.
But he has trouble deciding.

"Which sauce would you like to try?
Marinara sauce or alfredo sauce?"
JJ's grandma asks.

Cody chooses the creamy alfredo sauce. But JJ is unsure. He has never tried that kind of sauce before, and he doesn't know if he will like it. His grandma lets him try a spoonful.

JJ smiles. The sauce is delicious!

Now it's time for Cece to choose a pasta topping.

♪ There's tomatoes or bell peppers, olives chopped or onions diced. Pasta everywhere! It's up to you—which do you like? ♪

JJ's grandma offers Cece two choices. "Would you like to add tomatoes or black olives?" she asks Cece.

"I choose black olives," Cece says.

♪ White alfredo with black olives
on our noodles called bow ties!
Pasta everywhere!
We made it just the way we like! ♪

Soon the pasta is ready. Cece, JJ, and Cody can't wait to try it!

A few minutes later, JJ's mommy and daddy arrive. Everyone agrees that the pasta is super yummy!

JJ and his friends had a great day trying new foods and taking turns picking what they liked. They can't wait to have another pasta party soon!

If you had a pasta party with your friends, what kind of pasta would you have? Long spaghetti? Or wavy noodles? Would you add tomato sauce? Or yummy cheese? You can make it just the way you like!